SLICE OF MALLOW
ADAM FOREMAN
FOREMAN SLICE OF MALLOW
FOREMAN SLICE OF MALLOW

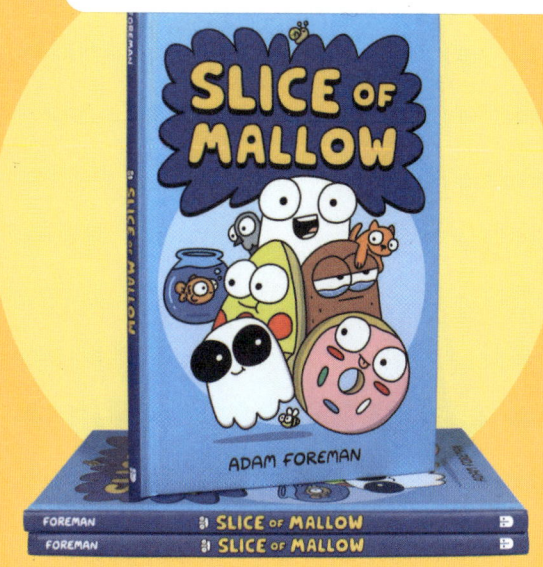

"SLICE OF MALLOW IS A SUPER SWEET, FUN-FILLED TREAT."

—JAMES BURKS, CREATOR OF *BIRD & SQUIRREL* GRAPHIC NOVELS

"SO FUN AND DELIGHTFULLY DRAWN!"

—JARRETT LERNER, AWARD-WINNING CREATOR OF *THE HUNGER HEROES* SERIES

"ABSOLUTELY CHARMING, FUNNY, AND SUPER CUTE ENTRY-LEVEL COMIC BOOK."

—PHIL CORBETT, CREATOR OF THE *KITTY QUEST* GRAPHIC NOVELS

"WITH CUTE CHARACTERS THAT LEAP RIGHT OFF THE PAGE, THIS BOOK REALLY KNOWS HOW TO ENGAGE WITH YOUNG READERS."

—ARON NELS STEINKE, EISNER-WINNING CARTOONIST AND CREATOR OF *MR. WOLF'S CLASS* SERIES

SLICE OF MALLOW
SECOND SLICE

ADAM FOREMAN

Andrews McMeel
PUBLISHING®

"FOR NIKKI AND FINN."

A BIG THANKS TO ERINN PASCAL FOR MAKING THE SLICE OF MALLOW GRAPHIC NOVELS HAPPEN AND FOR THE EXCELLENT EDITORIAL WISDOM. THANK YOU TO MARIA VICENTE FOR BEING THE BEST LITERARY AGENT A CARTOONIST COULD ASK FOR. THANKS TO NICOLA WELBOURNE FOR BEING SO HELPFUL AND SUPPORTIVE EVERY STEP OF THE WAY. SHOUTOUT TO THE CHILDREN AT OUTBURST OUT OF SCHOOL CLUB FOR INSPIRING ME TO CREATE CHILDREN'S COMICS. THANK YOU TO MY SUPER SUPPORTIVE FAMILY AND FRIENDS, ESPECIALLY FOR GIFTING ME MARSHMALLOWS EVERY BIRTHDAY! THANKS TO MY SON FINN, WHOSE INTERESTS INSPIRED LOTS OF TOPICS AND THEMES THROUGHOUT THE STORIES. THANK YOU TO ALL THE FRIENDS I'VE MADE ALONG THE WAY CREATING COMICS. LASTLY, A BIG THANKS TO YOU FOR READING THIS BOOK. THANK YOU!

© ADAM FOREMAN. ALL RIGHTS RESERVED. PRINTED IN CHINA. NO PART OF THIS BOOK MAY BE USED OR REPRODUCED IN ANY MANNER WHATSOEVER WITHOUT WRITTEN PERMISSION EXCEPT IN THE CASE OF REPRINTS IN THE CONTEXT OF REVIEWS.

ANDREWS MCMEEL PUBLISHING
A DIVISION OF ANDREWS MCMEEL UNIVERSAL
1130 WALNUT STREET, KANSAS CITY, MISSOURI 64106

WWW.ANDREWSMCMEEL.COM

25 26 27 28 29 SDB 10 9 8 7 6 5 4 3 2 1

ISBN: 978-1-5248-8084-2

LIBRARY OF CONGRESS CONTROL NUMBER: 2024944893

MADE BY:
RR DONNELLEY (GUANGDONG) PRINTING SOLUTIONS COMPANY LTD
ADDRESS AND LOCATION OF MANUFACTURER:
NO. 2, MINZHU ROAD, DANING, HUMEN TOWN,
DONGGUAN CITY, GUANGDONG PROVINCE, CHINA 523930
1ST PRINTING — 12/9/24

MIX
Paper | Supporting responsible forestry
FSC® C144853

ANDREWS MCMEEL PUBLISHING IS COMMITTED TO THE RESPONSIBLE USE OF NATURAL RESOURCES AND IS DEDICATED TO UNDERSTANDING, MEASURING, AND REDUCING THE IMPACT OF OUR PRODUCTS ON THE NATURAL WORLD. BY CHOOSING THIS PRODUCT, YOU ARE SUPPORTING RESPONSIBLE MANAGEMENT OF THE WORLD'S FORESTS. THE FSC® LABEL MEANS THAT THE MATERIALS USED FOR THIS PRODUCT COME FROM WELL-MANAGED FSC®-CERTIFIED FORESTS, RECYCLED MATERIALS, AND OTHER CONTROLLED SOURCES.

ATTENTION: SCHOOLS AND BUSINESSES
ANDREWS MCMEEL BOOKS ARE AVAILABLE AT QUANTITY DISCOUNTS WITH BULK PURCHASE FOR EDUCATIONAL, BUSINESS, OR SALES PROMOTIONAL USE. FOR INFORMATION, PLEASE EMAIL THE ANDREWS MCMEEL PUBLISHING SPECIAL SALES DEPARTMENT: SALES@ANDREWSMCMEEL.COM.

HI, I'M MALLOW!
I KNOW.
HELLO, I'M PIZZA!
I KNOW!
I ALREADY KNOW WHO YOU BOTH ARE.
WE ARE TALKING TO THE READER.
?

Panel 1:
- OH, WELL MY NAME IS...
- WOW! LOOK AT WHAT'S BEHIND YOU PIZZA!
- ?

Panel 2:
- ≡HUMPH≡
- WHAT?
- WHAT'S BEHIND ME?

Panel 3:
- I SAID, MY NAME IS...
- YAY! OUR DELIVERY HAS ARRIVED!

LET'S GO AND OPEN IT!
HUFF
FINALLY.
MY NAME IS...
ARE YOU COMING WITH US?
MY NAME IS JELLY!

FINE, SHOW ME THIS AMAZING DELIVERY.
TRAM-PO-LEEN!
OKAY, THAT IS COOL.
WE HAVE THREE FUN STORIES FOR YOU, READER.
BUT FIRST...
JUMP!

BOING!
WOW!
SO MUCH AIR!
PFFT, THAT'S EASY TO DO.
TRIPLE FLIP!
EPIC!
THAT IS **ALSO** EASY TO DO.
...PROBABLY.
YOU'RE AMAZING, MALLOW!

EVERYONE THINKS MALLOW IS SO GREAT!

MALLOW, MALLOW, MALLOW! IT'S **ALWAYS** ABOUT MALLOW.

ARE YOU OKAY, JELLY?

8

ANYTHING MALLOW CAN DO, I CAN DO BETTER!

IF YOU THINK THAT WAS A GOOD JUMP...
WATCH THIS!

BE CAREFUL, JELLY!
JUMP!
NONSENSE!

I KNEW I COULD JUMP BETTER THAN MALLOW!
MEGA BOUNCE!
JELLY IS JUMPING ALL THE WAY TO THE FIRST STORY.

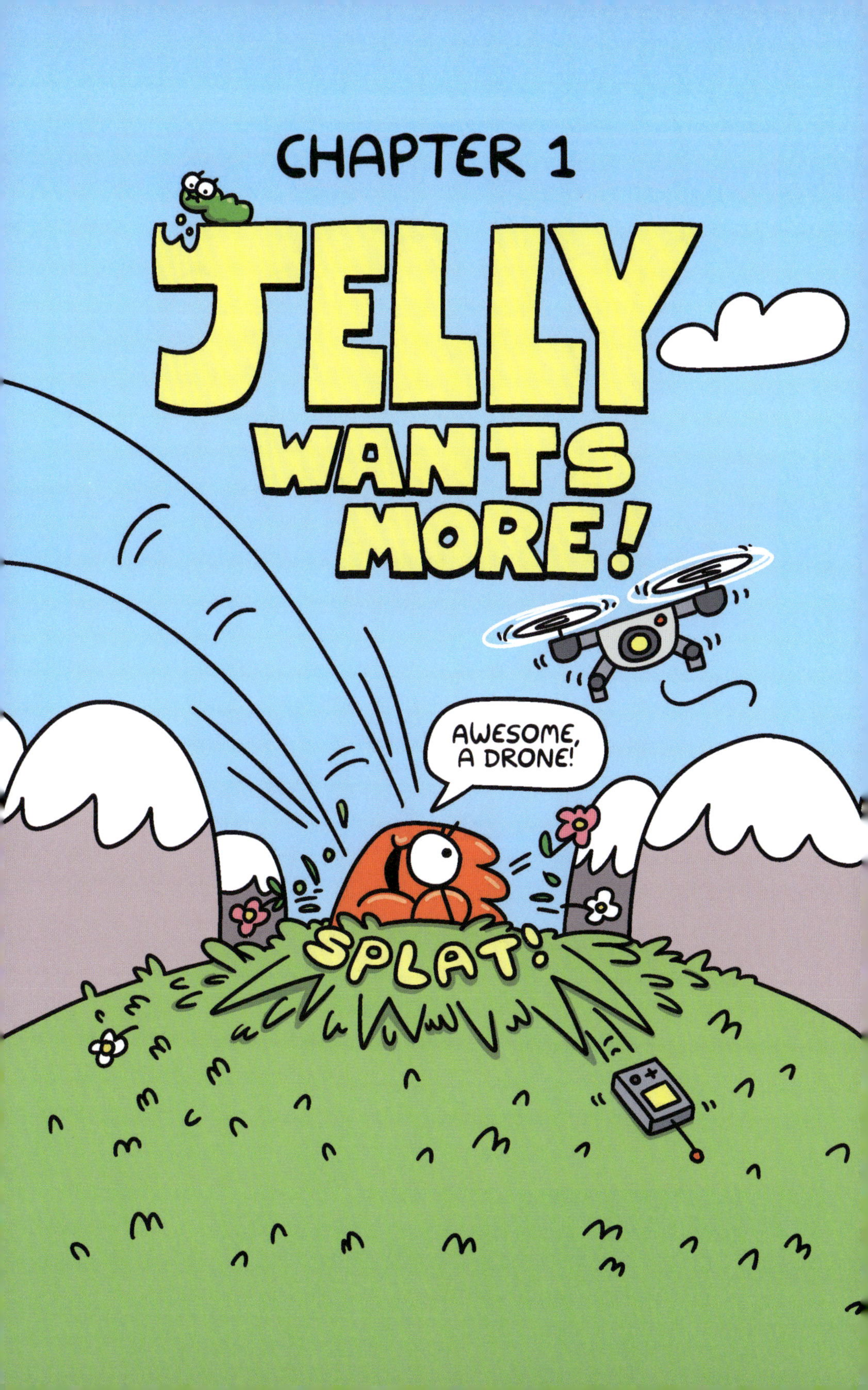
CHAPTER 1
JELLY WANTS MORE!
AWESOME, A DRONE!
SPLAT!

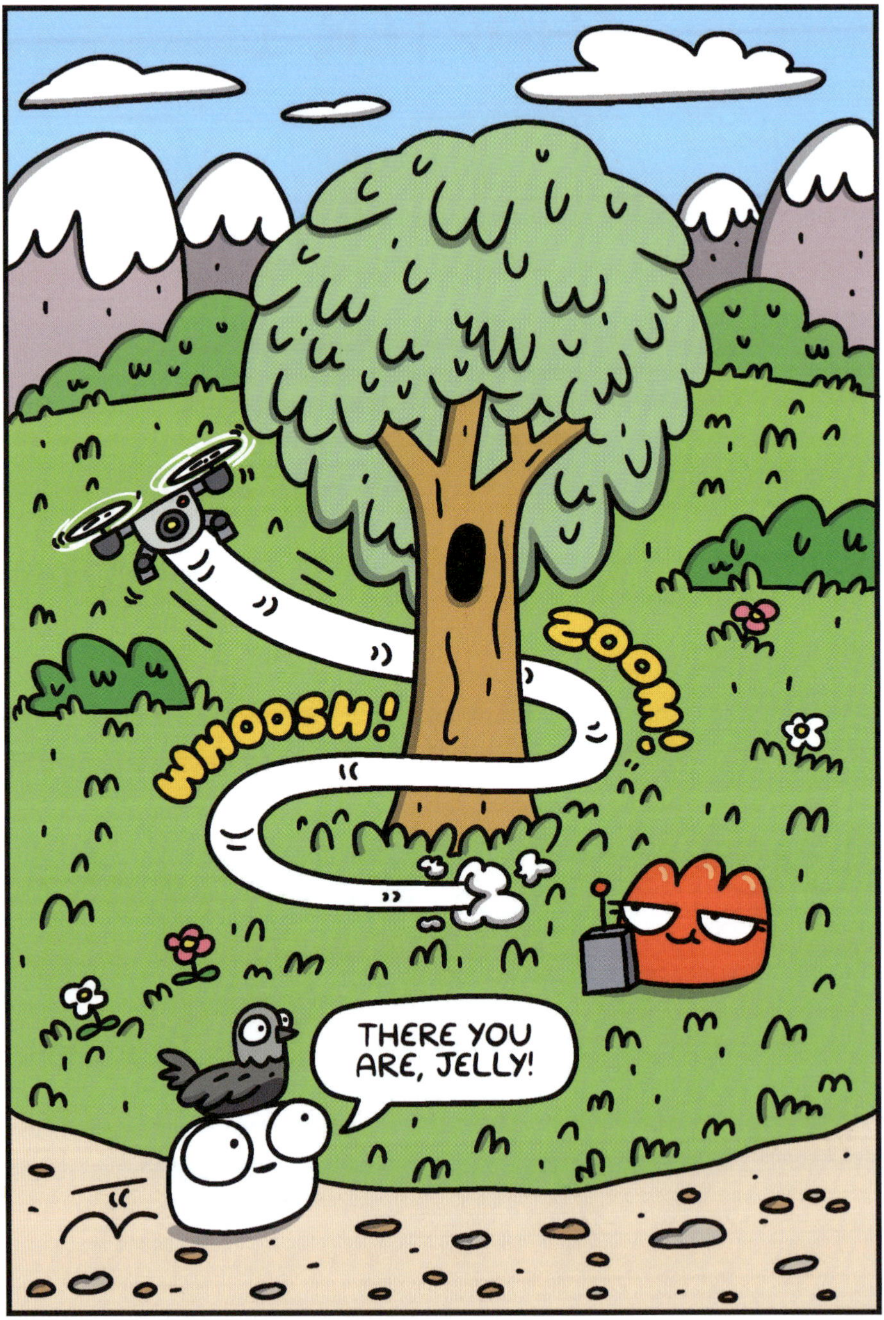
WHOOSH!
ZOOM!
THERE YOU ARE, JELLY!

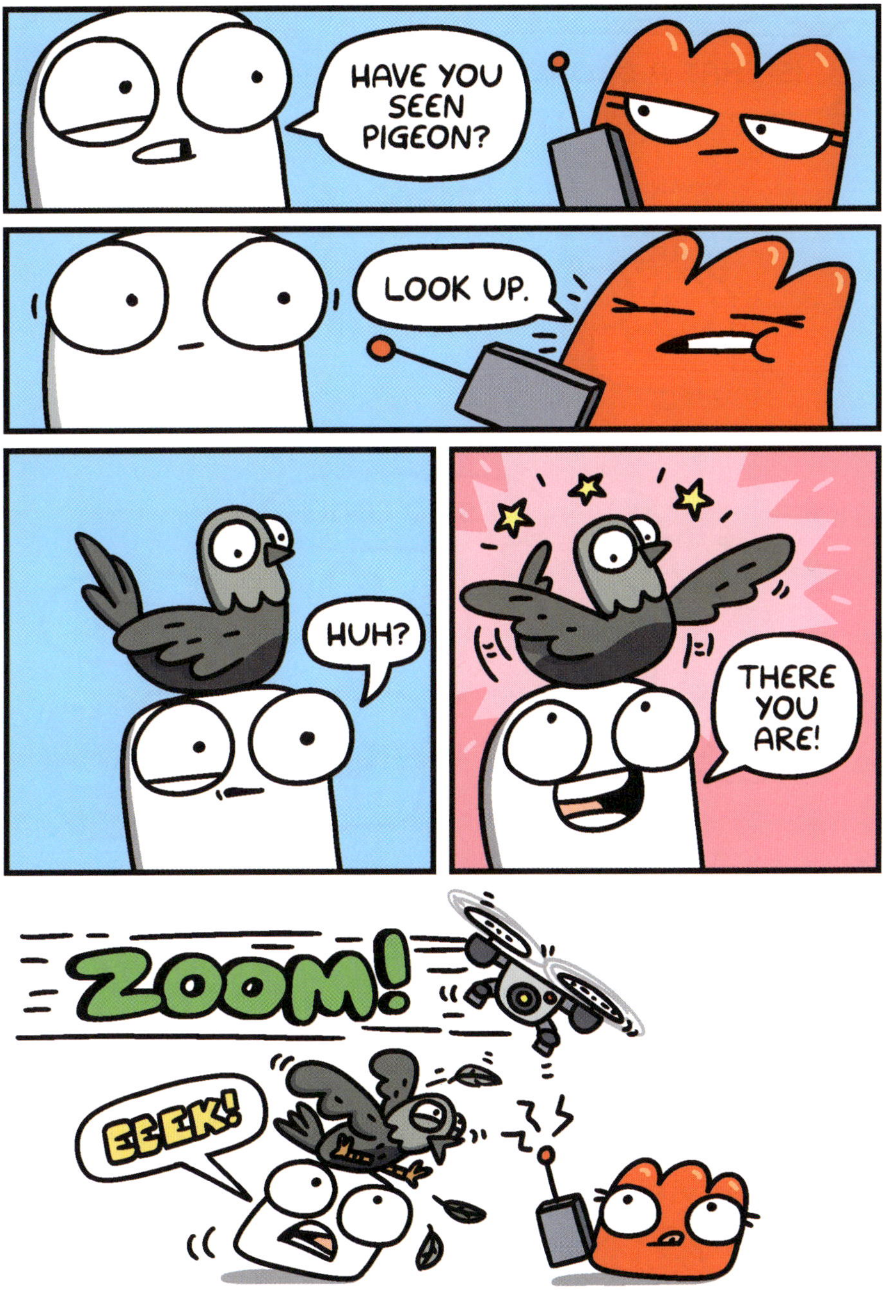
HAVE YOU SEEN PIGEON?
LOOK UP.
HUH?
THERE YOU ARE!
ZOOM!
EEEK!

IS THAT A DRONE?
YES.
IT'S SO COOL!
I KNOW.
WHOOSH!
CAN I HAVE A GO?
NO.
YOU WILL PROBABLY CRASH IT.

CRASH! ZOOM!

NOOOO!

MY DRONE.

IT'S STUCK!
THAT WAS **IMPRESSIVE.** HOW DID YOU FLY IT LIKE THAT?
IMPRESSIVE?
HMMM.
YES. I DID IT ON PURPOSE.
...BUT NOW I CAN'T GET IT BACK OUT!

DO YOU THINK YOU CAN HELP, PIGEON?
COO COO!
WHOOSH!
CREAK!
PECK! PECK!
FALL!
I CAN'T BELIEVE THAT WORKED.

GREAT WORK, PIGEON!
YOU'RE THE BEST PET EVER!
SO CUTE!
PFFT, MY PET IS BETTER AND MUCH MORE ADORABLE!
THROW!
YOU HAVE A PET, JELLY?
ERR.
YES, AND I'M TOTALLY NOT LYING.

CAN I SEE?
YES, OF COURSE. IT'S, ERR...
ROCK!
SCRIBBLE DOODLE
PERFECT.
HERE IT IS. MY PET ROCK.

EEEEEEK!
IT LOOKS SCARY!
WELL, I LIKE YOUR PET ROCK, JELLY.
COO?!
IT CAN FLY TOO!
THROW!
WATCH THIS!

SEE, I TOLD YOU MY PET IS BETTER.
WATCH OUT!
?!
SPLAT!
WHAT HAPPENED? WHERE DID MY PET ROCK GO?

HA HA HA HA!
INSIDE OF YOU!
IT'S STUCK!
HOW WILL I GET IT OUT?
?
WHAT ARE YOU LOOKING AT?
COO.
PECK!

I THINK PIGEON IS JUST TRYING TO HELP BY GETTING YOUR PET ROCK FOR YOU.
PECK! PECK! PECK! PECK! PECK! PECK! PECK! PECK!
PIGEON IS SO CUTE!
IT'S A NICE DAY, DO YOU WANT TO GET SOME ICE CREAM?
YES!
LET'S GO, YOU TWO!
PECK!

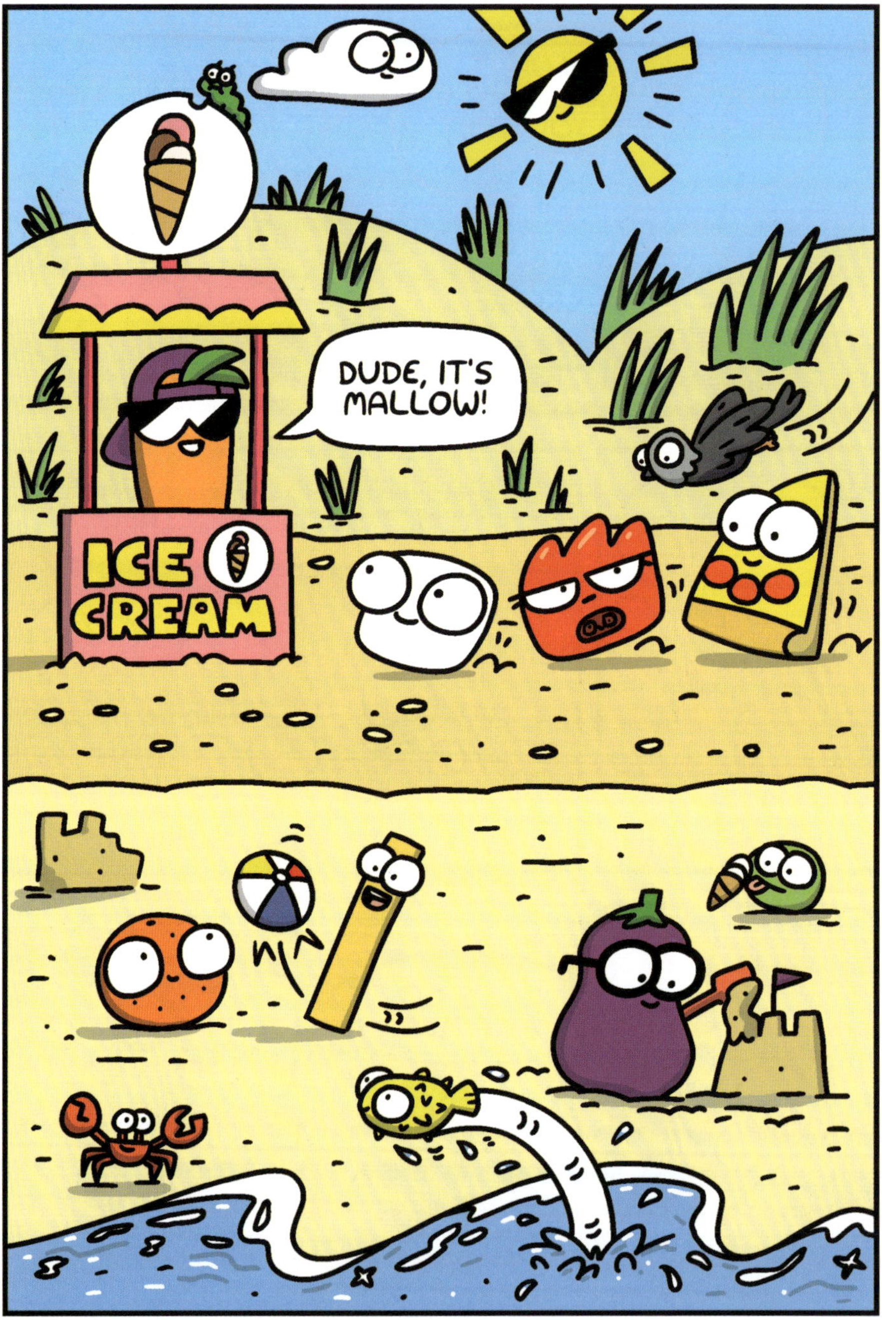
ICE CREAM
DUDE, IT'S MALLOW!

HI, CARROT. THREE SCOOPS OF ICE CREAM, PLEASE.
ICE CREA
MALLOW GOT THREE SCOOPS OF ICE CREAM?
FOUR SCOOPS OF ICE CREAM FOR ME, PLEASE.
ICE CREAM
NO, ACTUALLY...
MAKE IT THIRTY SCOOPS!

ARE YOU FOR REAL? THAT'S A LOT OF ICE CREAM!
YES!
ANYTHING MALLOW DOES, **I CAN DO BETTER.**
WHAT DID YOU SAY?
EEEEK! ...NOTHING.
HERE YOU GO, DUDE!
THROW!
IT'S PERFECT!

I WILL EAT MINE EVEN FASTER THAN MALLOW!
YUM!
WATCH THIS!
LICK!
MUNCH!
JUMP!
SLURP!
MUNCH! MUNCH!

ALL GONE!

?!

UGGH!

BRAIN FREEZE!

ARE YOU OK?
!
LICK
PUKE!
HA HA HA!
WELL AT LEAST YOUR PET ROCK ISN'T STUCK INSIDE YOU ANYMORE.
THROW!

I TRIED TO BE BETTER THAN MALLOW AT EVERYTHING, BUT I FAILED.
WHAT. WHY?
ICE CREAM
I JUST WANT EVERYONE TO LIKE ME, LIKE THEY LIKE YOU.
I WANT MY OWN BOOK TOO CALLED *SLICE OF JELLY.*
THIS WHOLE BOOK HAS BEEN ABOUT YOU SO FAR, JELLY.
REALLY?
YEAH, BUT...

JUST THE FIRST CHAPTER.
THANK YOU SO MUCH.
I'VE GOT SO MANY IDEAS WE CAN DO FOR IT!
IT'S THE END OF THE CHAPTER NOW.
WHAT?!
NOOO!
EXCUSE ME, I DIDNT GET MY ICE CREAM.
ICE CREAM

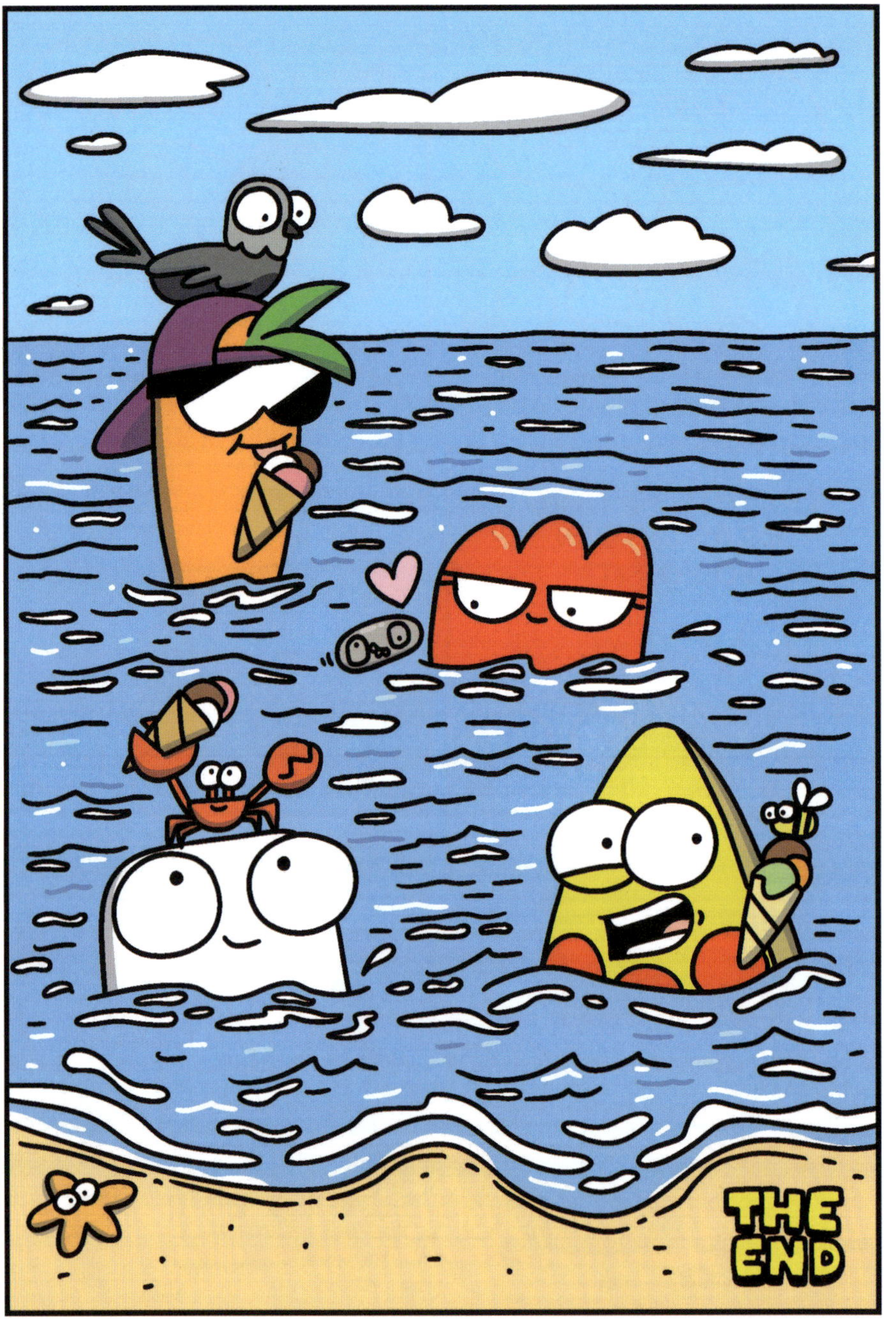
THE END

WHY ARE YOU UPSIDE DOWN, READER?
UNLESS...
I AM?
GULP!
CRASH!
THE NEXT STORY IS CALLED...

SUPER SMILE

CHAPTER 2

?!

JUMP!

WHAT'S WITH THE DRAMATIC JUMPING, MALLOW?

I'M A SUPERHERO TODAY!

A SUPER HERO?
AWESOME!
WHAT A TERRIBLE IDEA.
HMMM.
I COULD BE A BAD GUY TODAY!
BYE! ...FOR NOW!
WHAT ABOUT YOUR HOT CHOCOLATE, JELLY?

SUPERHEROES HAVE SUPER POWERS.
SIP
WHAT'S YOURS, MALLOW?
SUPERHERO EGG! THE MOVIE!
I HAVE A SUPER SMILE!
SMILES ARE SO POWERFUL.
IS THAT A SUPERPOWER?
YES, WATCH!

READY?
YUP.
SMILE
GIGGLE
SEE! YOU SMILED TOO!
WOW! THAT REALLY IS A POWERFUL SUPERPOWER.
ALERT! ALERT!
SUPERHERO EGG! THE MOVIE!
WHAT IS IT, PHONE?

YOU HAVE A NEW MESSAGE!
WHAT DOES IT SAY?
SIP
IT SAYS...
READING
"I'M GOING TO ROB A BANK AND YOU CAN'T STOP ME, MALLOW!"
WHAT?!
PFFF!

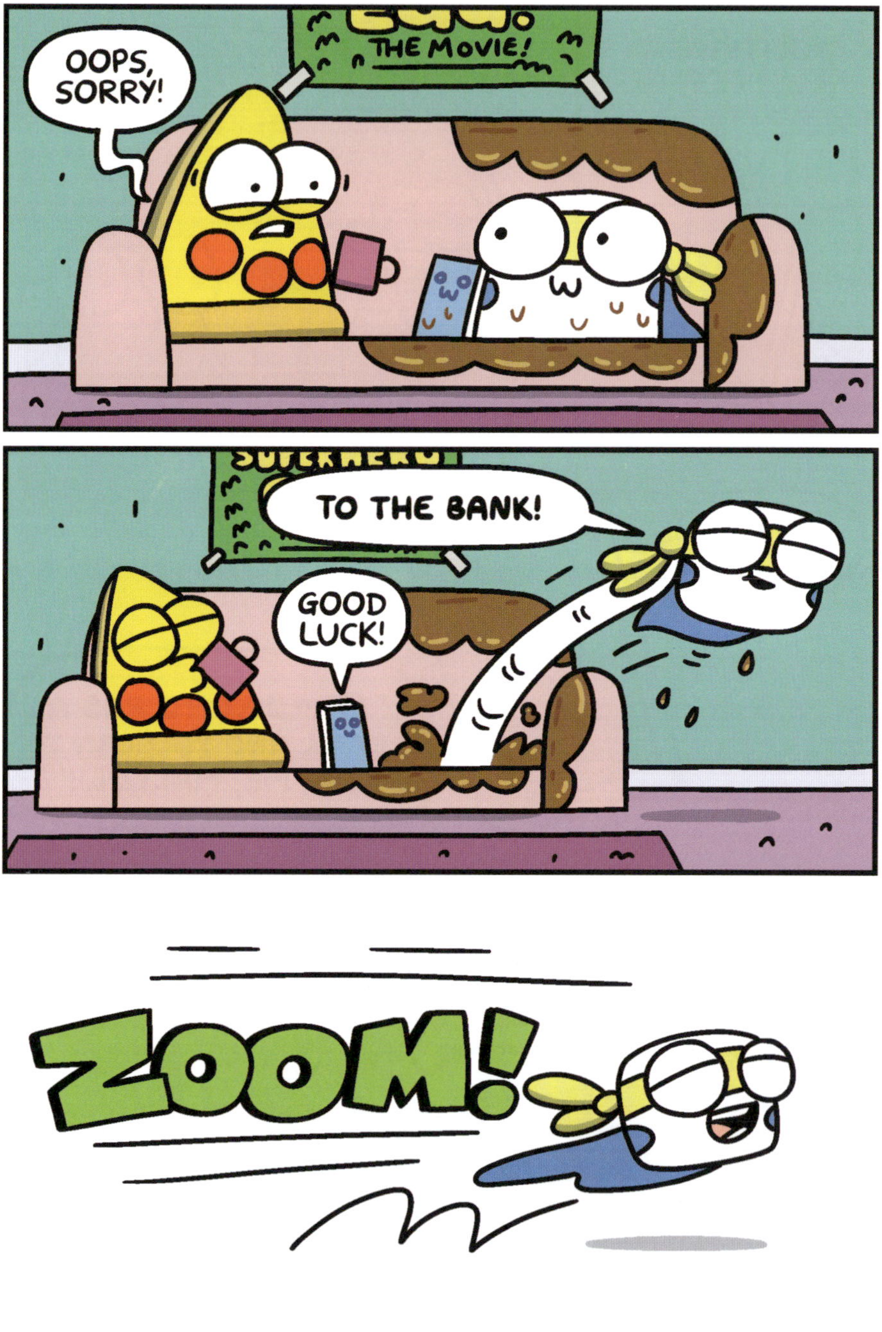
THE MOVIE!
OOPS, SORRY!
TO THE BANK!
GOOD LUCK!
ZOOM!

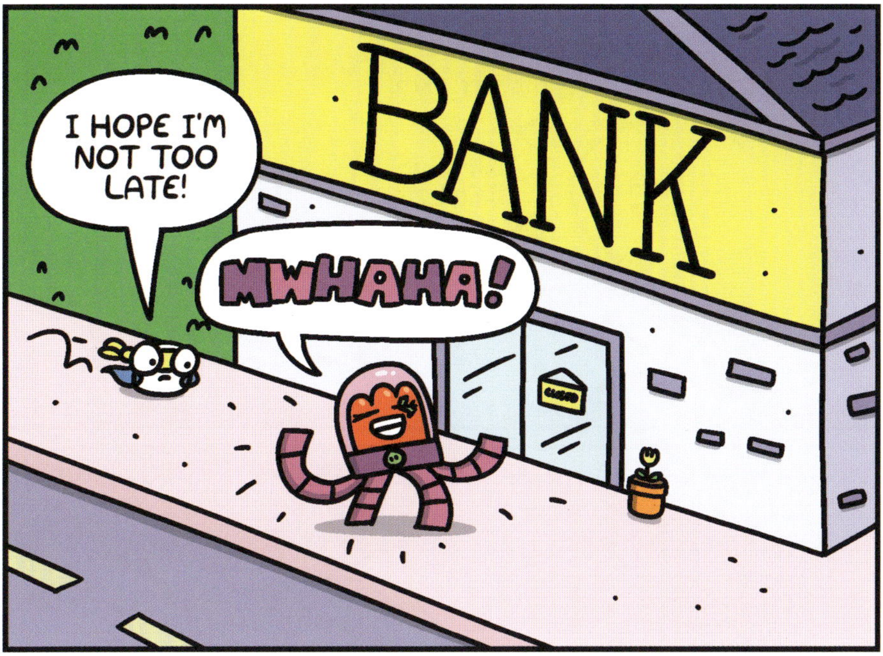
BANK
I HOPE I'M NOT TOO LATE!
MWHAHA!

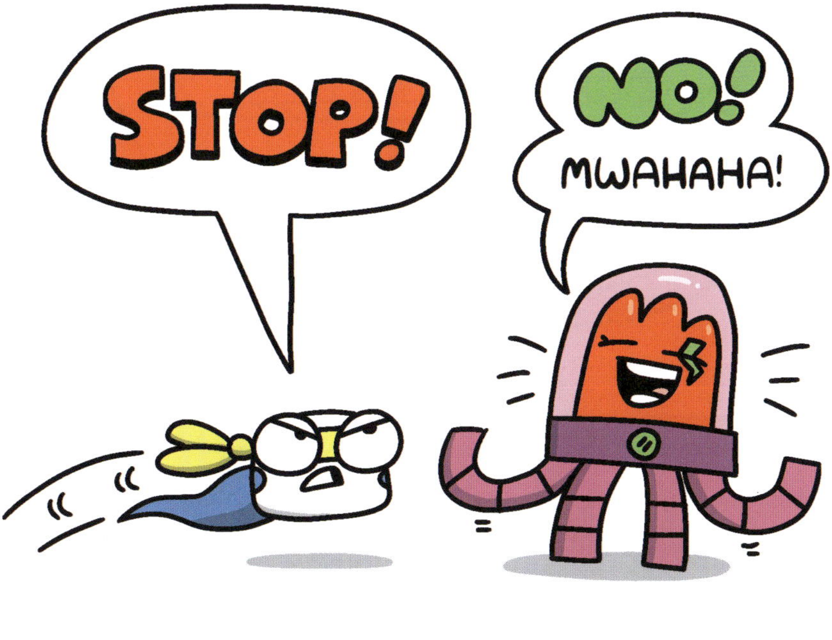
STOP!
NO!
MWAHAHA!

JELLY?
IS THAT YOU?
JELLY?!
WHO IS JELLY?
I DON'T KNOW WHO THIS JELLY IS, BUT SHE SOUNDS REALLY AWESOME!
I'M A BAD GUY WITH SUPER COOL ROBOT ARMS! MWHAHAHA!!
I KNOW IT'S YOU, JELLY.
BUSTED.

WELL, I'M ROBBING THE BANK ANYWAY. **JUST TRY AND STOP ME!**
OK!
THE BANK IS CLOSED TODAY, SO YOU CAN'T GET IN.
CLOSED
NOOO!

THEN I'M GOING TO SMASH THIS PLANT POT INSTEAD!
GASP!
YONK!
MWHAHA HAHA
SUPER SMILE
?!

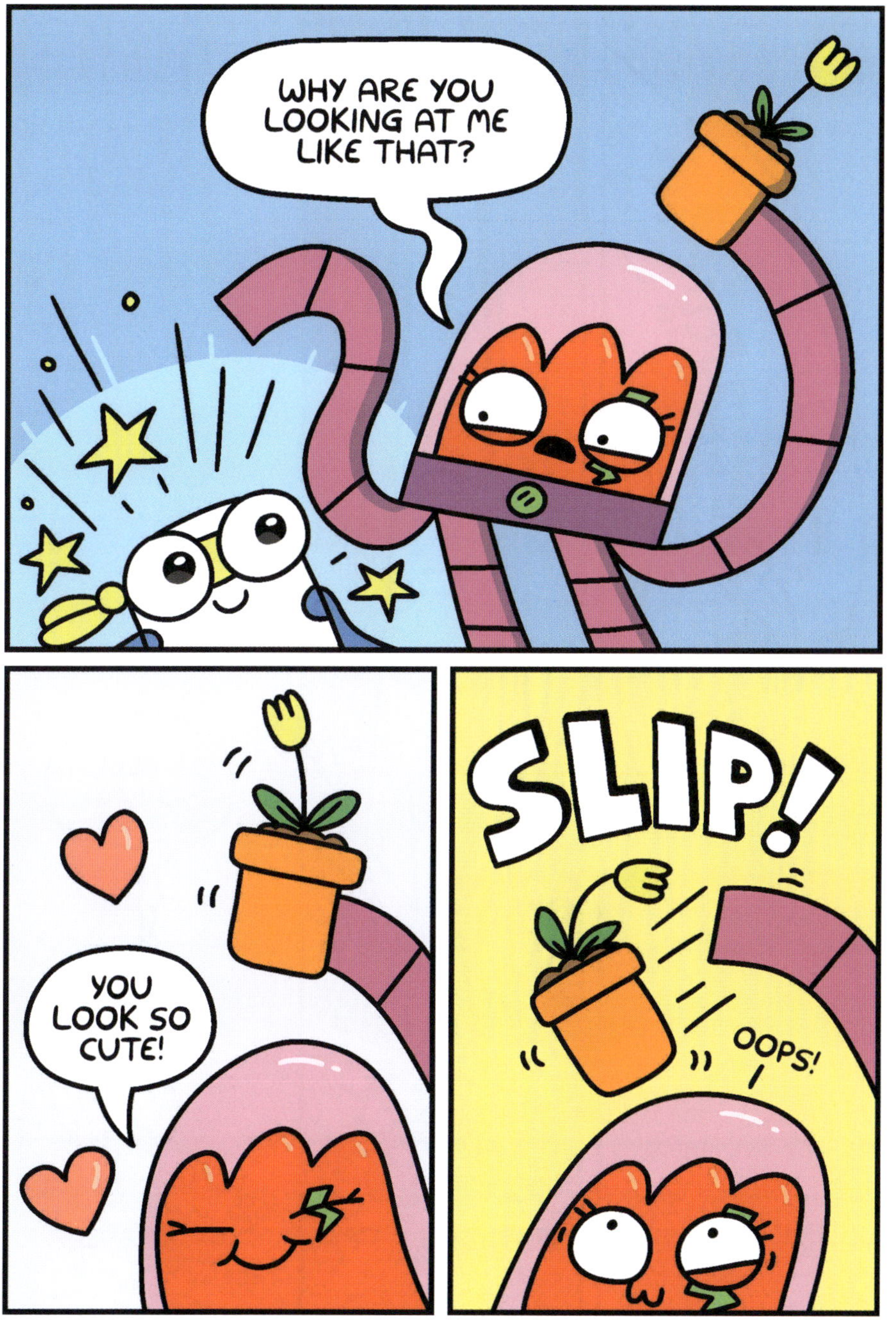
WHY ARE YOU LOOKING AT ME LIKE THAT?
YOU LOOK SO CUTE!
SLIP!
OOPS!

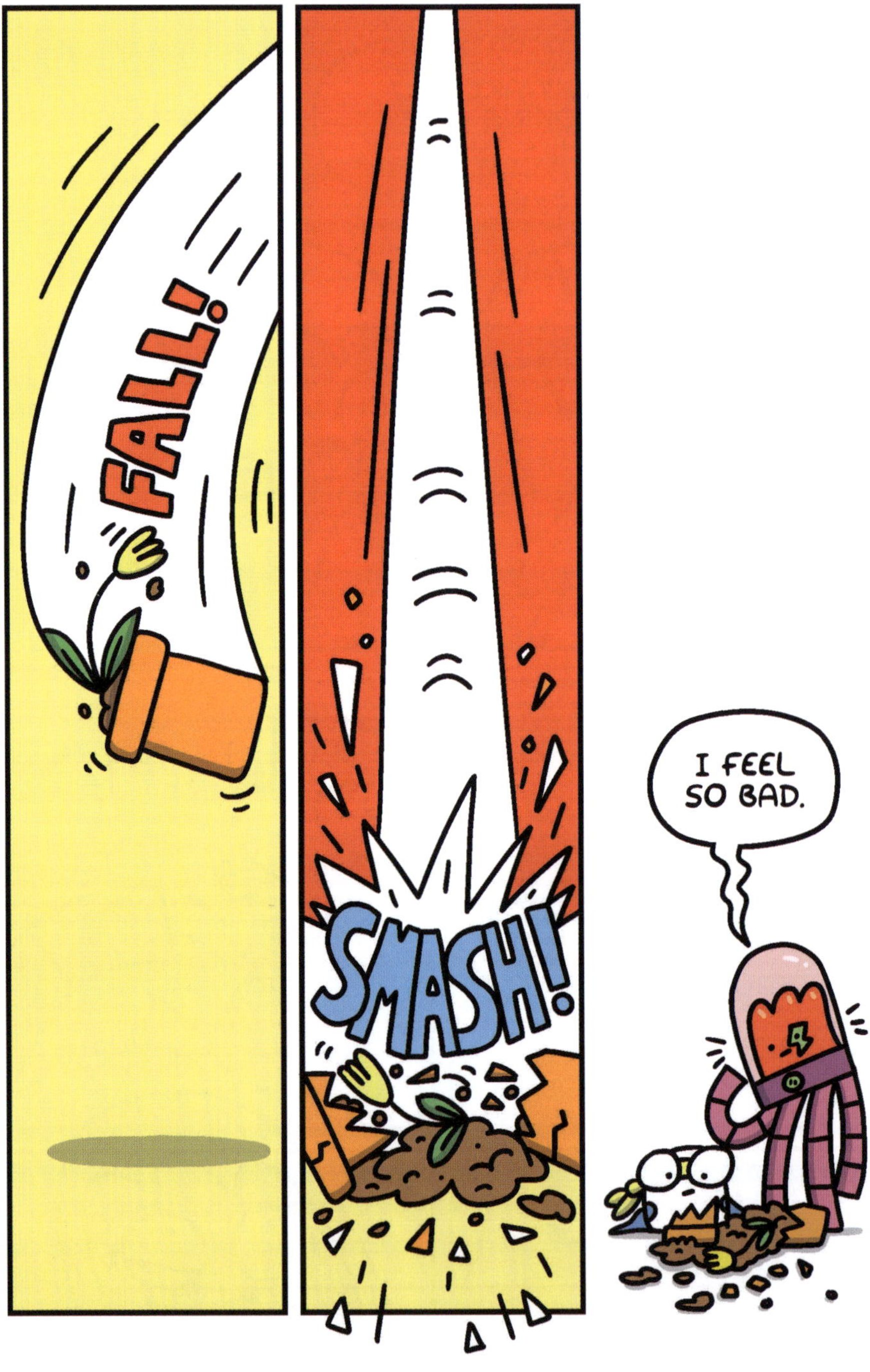
FALL!
SMASH!
I FEEL SO BAD.

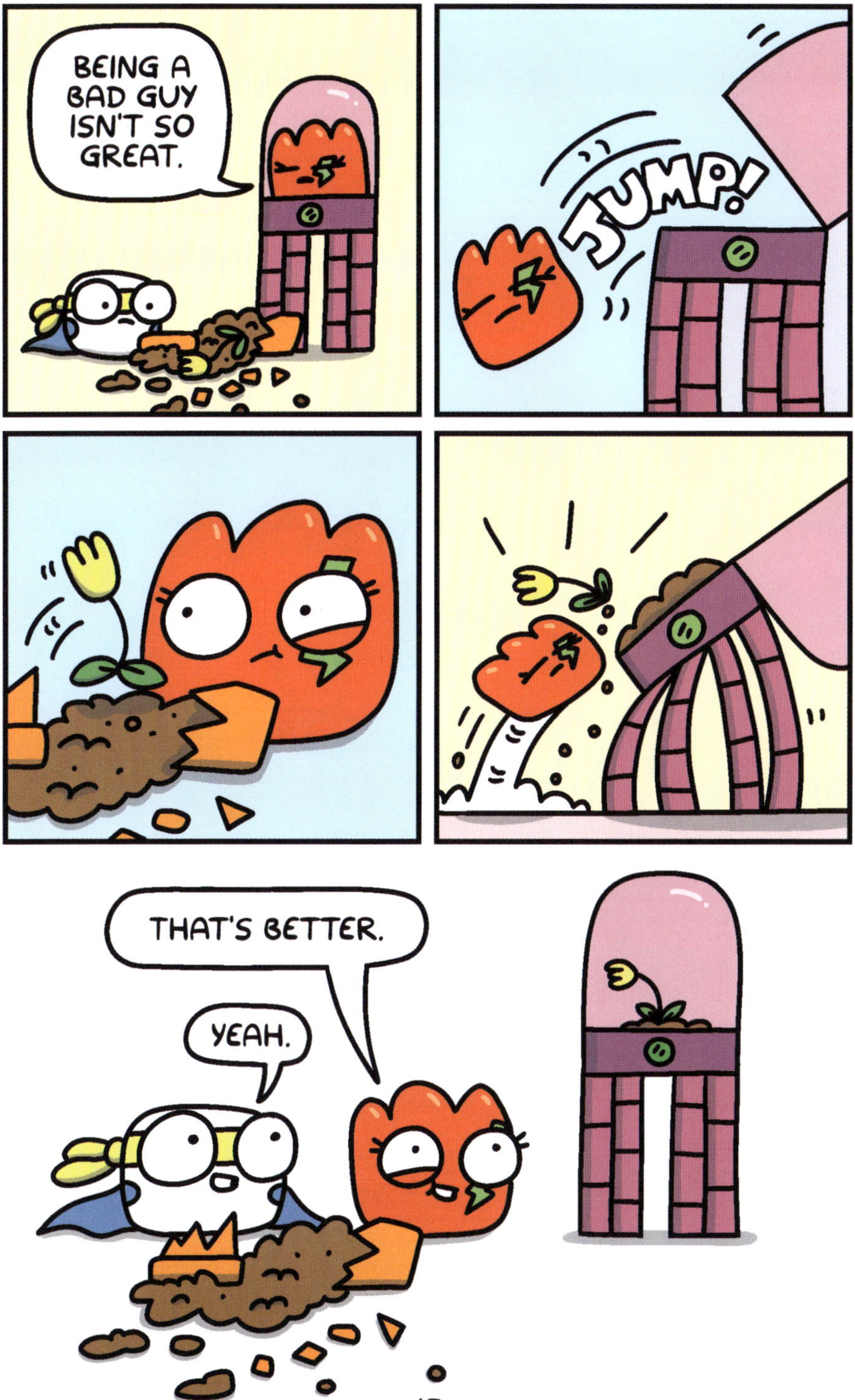
BEING A BAD GUY ISN'T SO GREAT.
JUMP!
THAT'S BETTER.
YEAH.

WHAT NOW?
I DON'T KNOW.
LET'S GET ICE CREAM!
!
BLEURGH!
NEVER AGAIN!
HOW ABOUT YOUR FAVORITE, HOT CHOCOLATE?
OK.
CLOSED

MWHAHAHA!

I'M GOING TO ROB ALL THE BANKS IN THE WORLD!

BANK

SMASH!

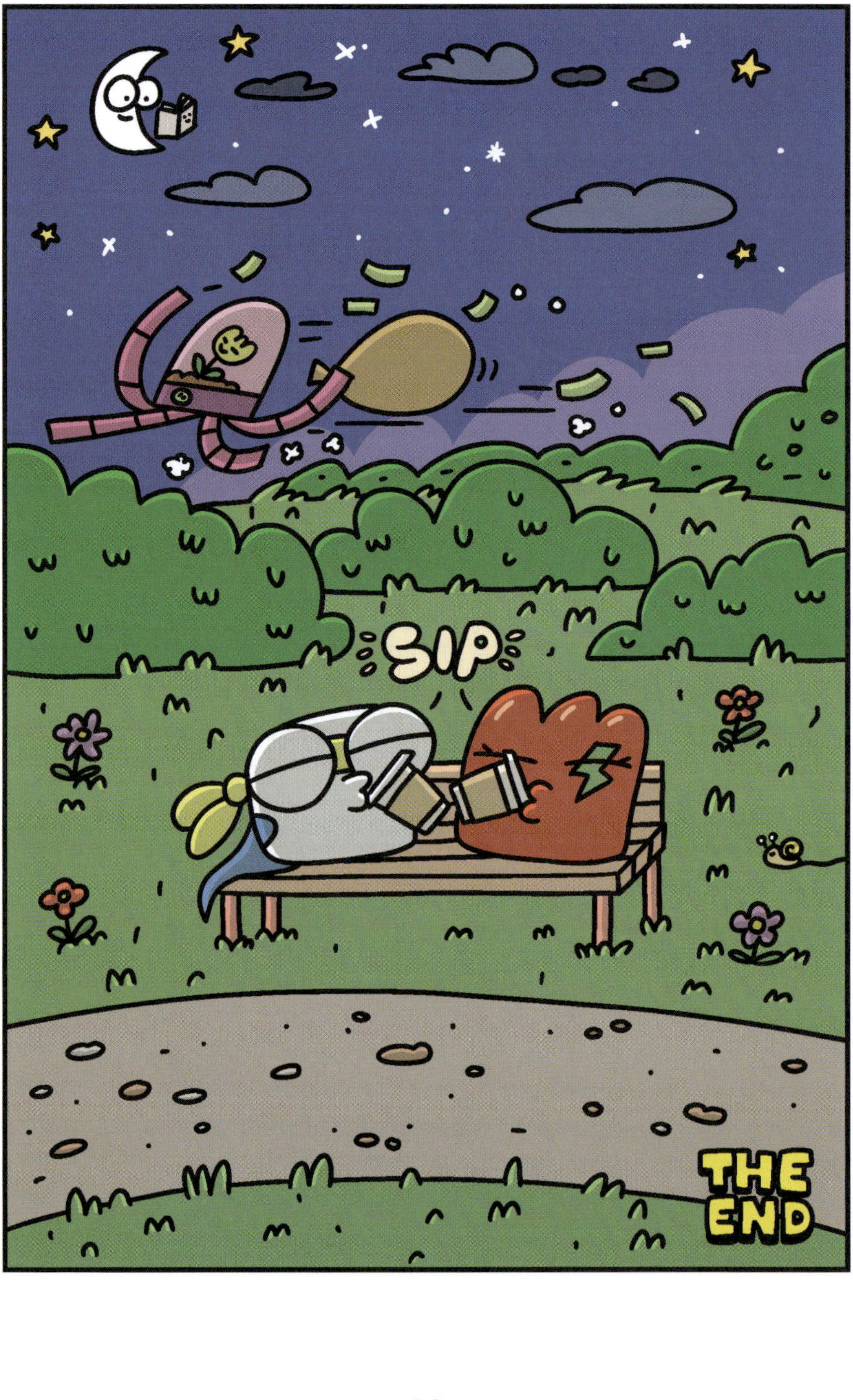
SIP
THE END

LOST ANYTHING, PIZZA?
?
WHERE IS YOUR PEPPERONI?
WELP!
GIGGLE
ZOOM!
HAHA!
THE NEXT STORY IS CALLED...

LOST

CHAPTER 3

WHERE ARE MALLOW AND PIZZA?
2
HAPPY BIRTHDAY JELLY!
THEY'RE LATE.
WHAT ARE THEY DOING THAT'S SO IMPORTANT?

HA HA HA!
SAY IT AGAIN!
SHAM-POO BOTTLE!
POO! HAHA!
HA HA HA!
JELLY WILL LOVE THIS GIFT.
HAHA
HAHA
HA
HA
HA

WE'RE SO LATE!
WE'RE GOING TO MISS JELLY'S BIRTHDAY PARTY!
I HAVE AN IDEA!
LET'S JUMP OUT OF THE COMIC AND GO TO THE PAGE WITH JELLY'S PARTY ON IT.
WHAT?

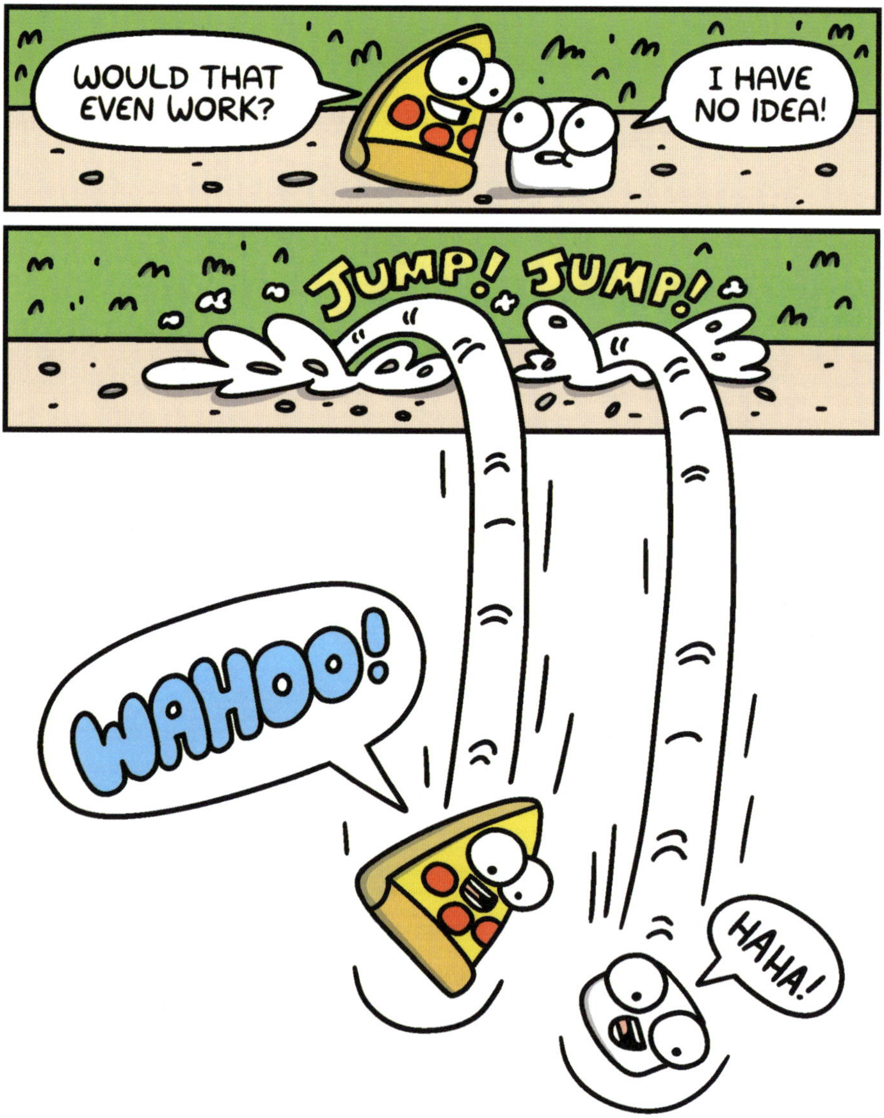
WOULD THAT EVEN WORK?
I HAVE NO IDEA!
JUMP! JUMP!
WAHOO!
HAHA!

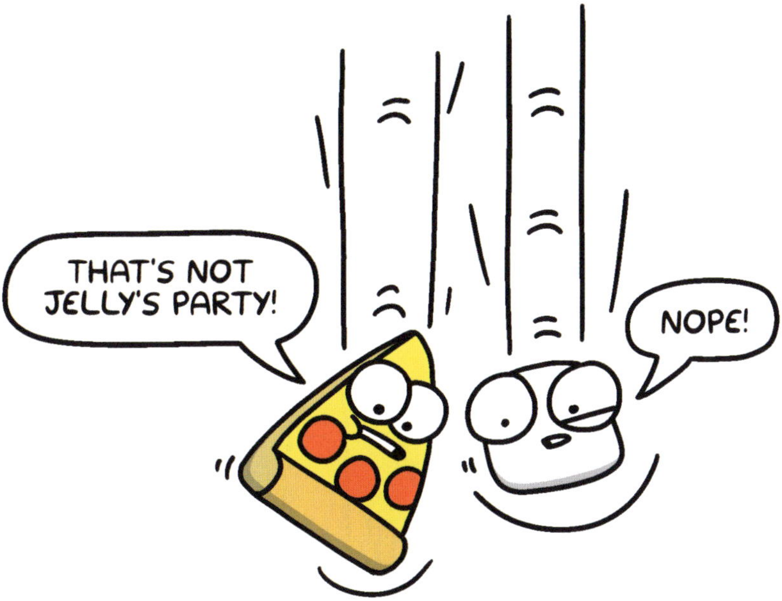
THAT'S NOT JELLY'S PARTY!
NOPE!

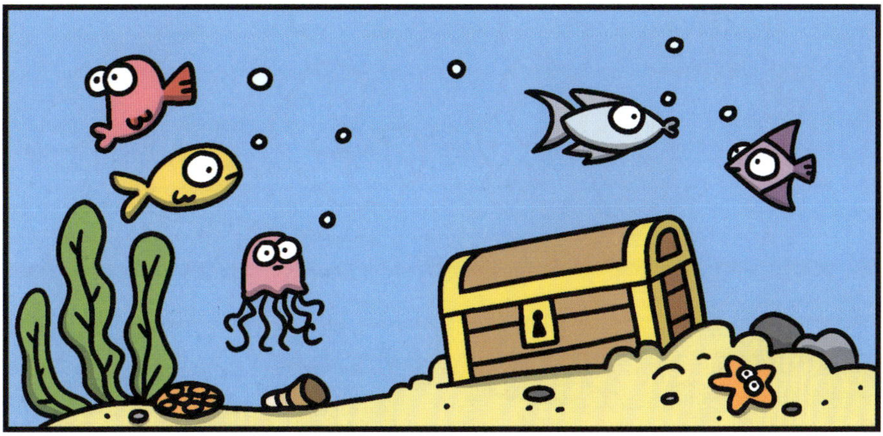

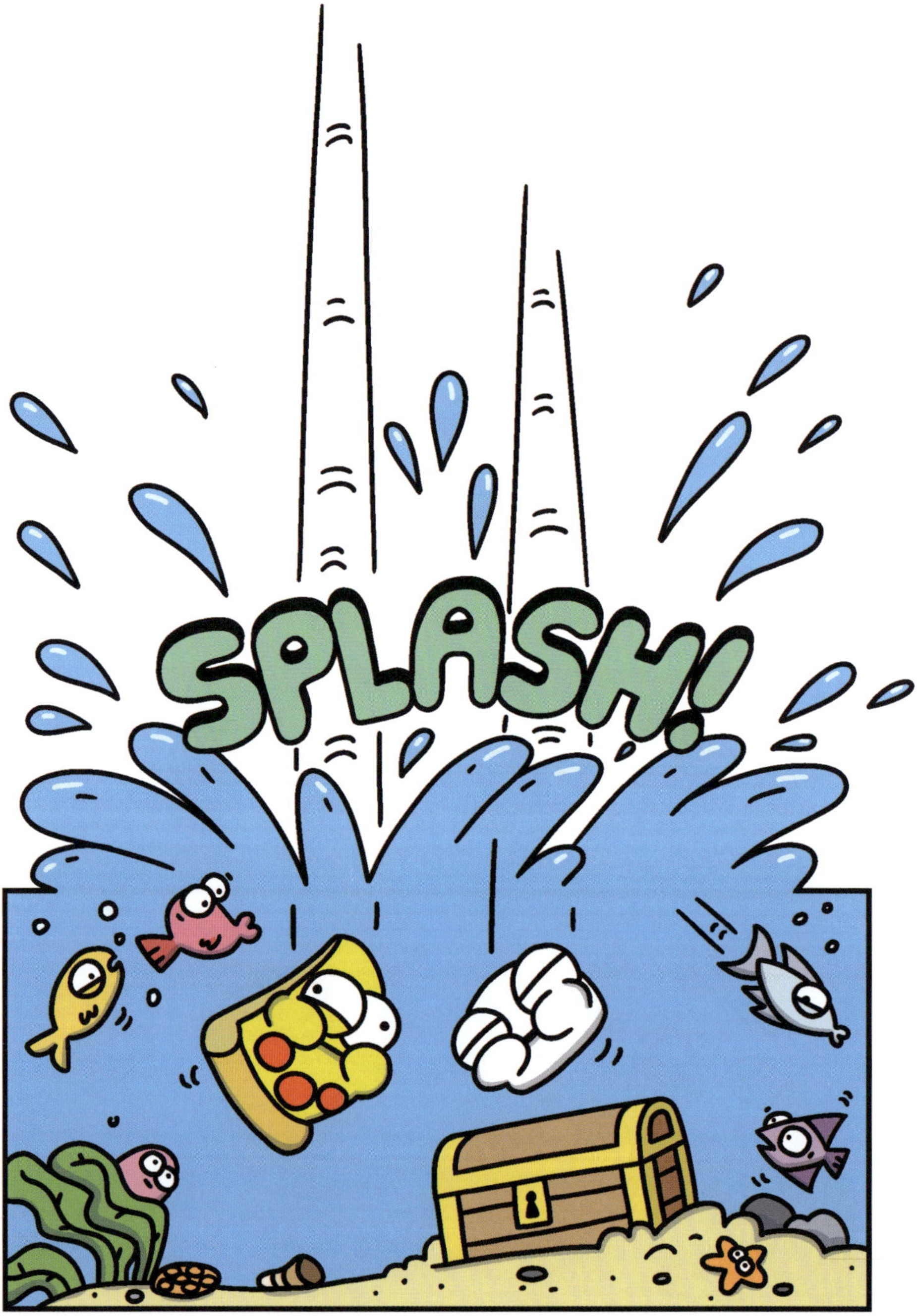
SPLASH!

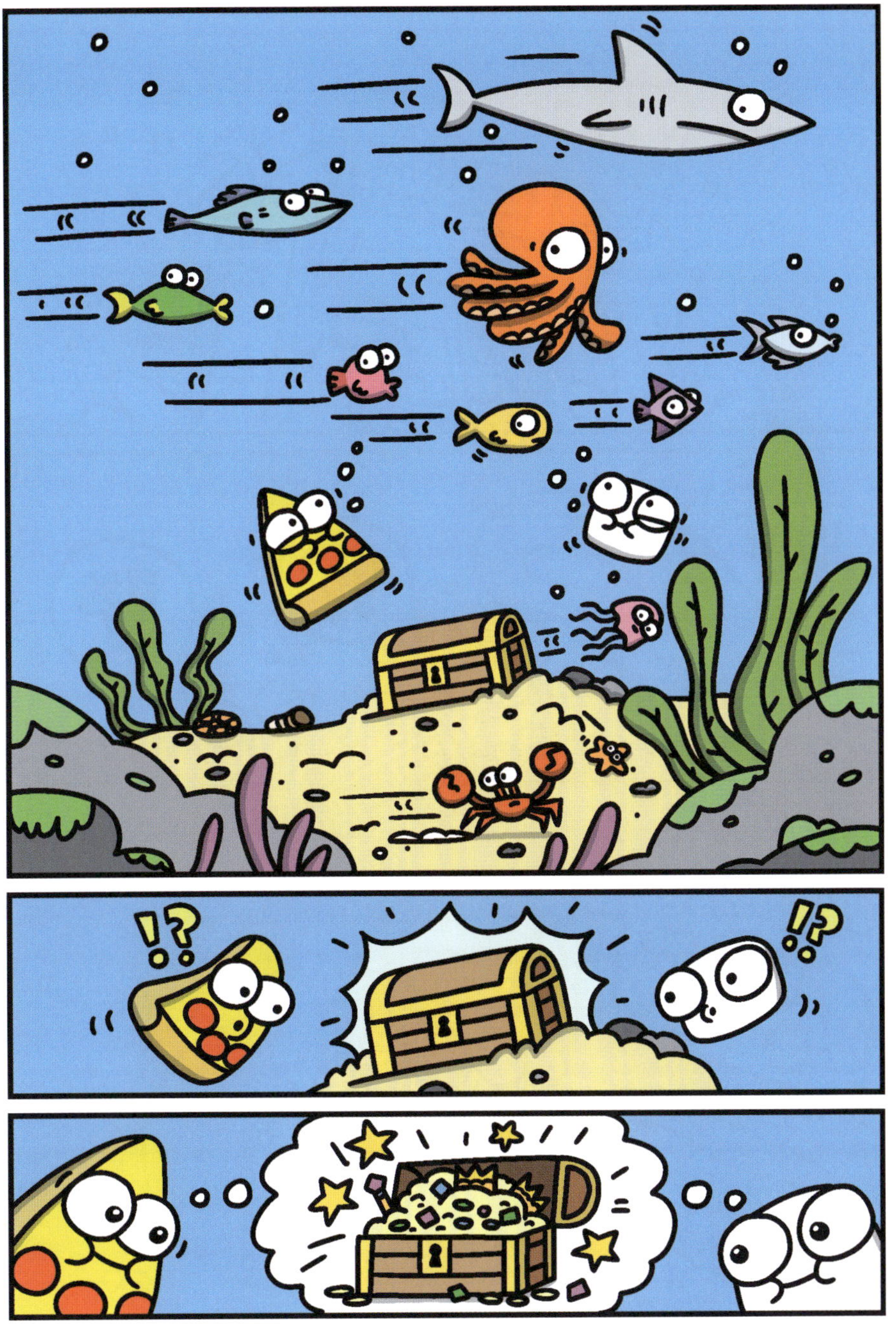
!?
!?

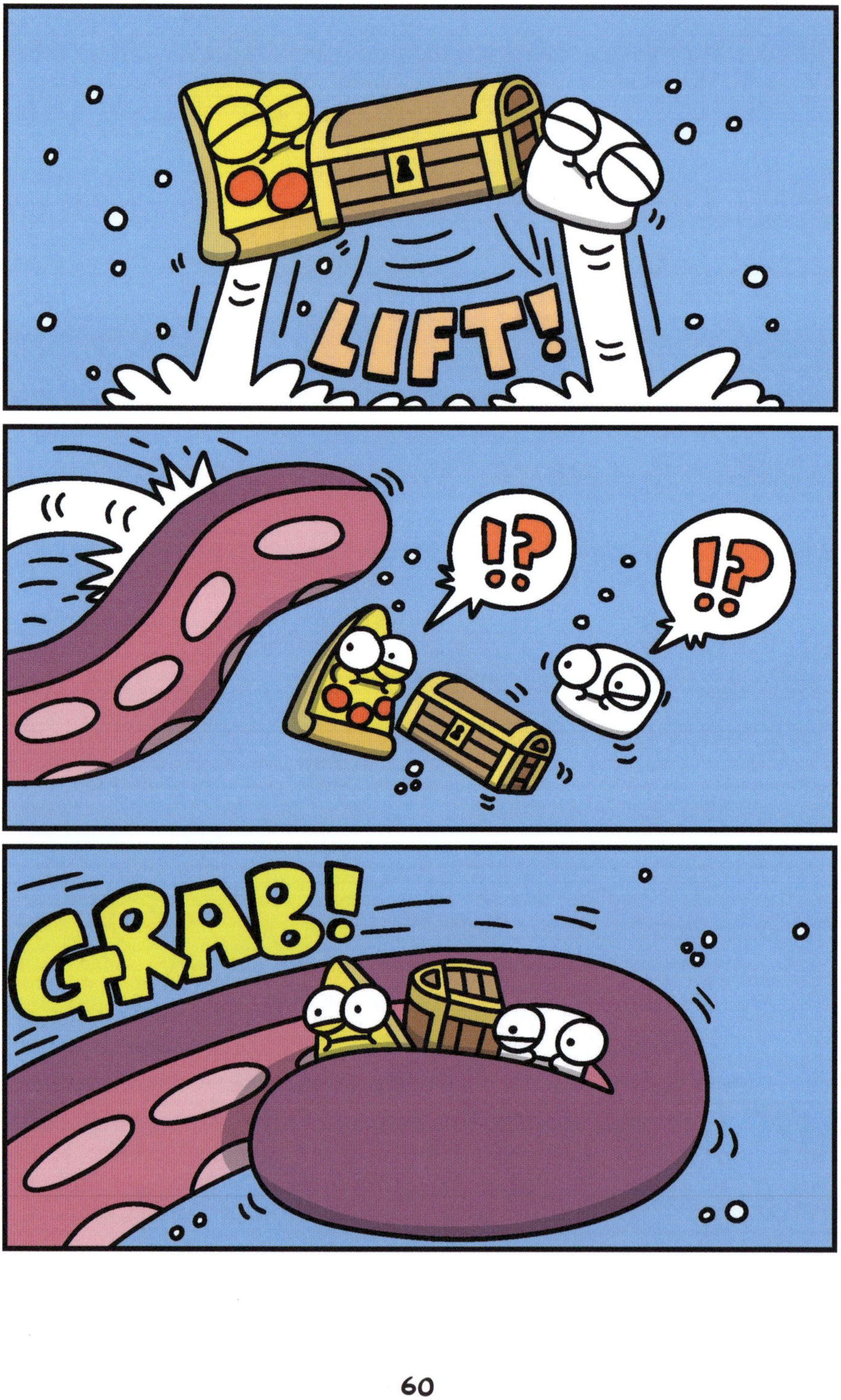
LIFT!
!?
!?
GRAB!

THROW!
THUD!
ARE YOU OK?
NO!
WHY DID WE JUMP OUT OF THE COMIC?! WE ARE SO LOST!

WE SHOULD BE AT JELLY'S PARTY, EATING CAKE!
NOT STUCK ON A DESERTED ISLAND WITH...
A GOLD CHEST!
GOLD!
OPEN!
COINS!
HI, LOSERS.
TOOT!

HAHA!
TOOT!
NO GOLD, NO CAKE. JUST ONE FARTING COIN.
DID YOU SAY CAKE? I LOVE CAKE!
WHERE IS THE CAKE!?
THERE IS CAKE AT JELLY'S BIRTHDAY PARTY?
YAY!
BUT WE'RE STUCK ON THIS TINY ISLAND SO WE CAN'T HAVE ANY.
TOOT!

I KNOW A WAY!
YOU DO?
WE JUMP OUT OF THE COMIC, TO THE PAGE WITH CAKE!
WE TRIED JUMPING OUT OF THE COMIC BEFORE. IT'S HOW WE ENDED UP LOST HERE.
OH.
SO NO CAKE?
IT'S WORTH ANOTHER TRY.

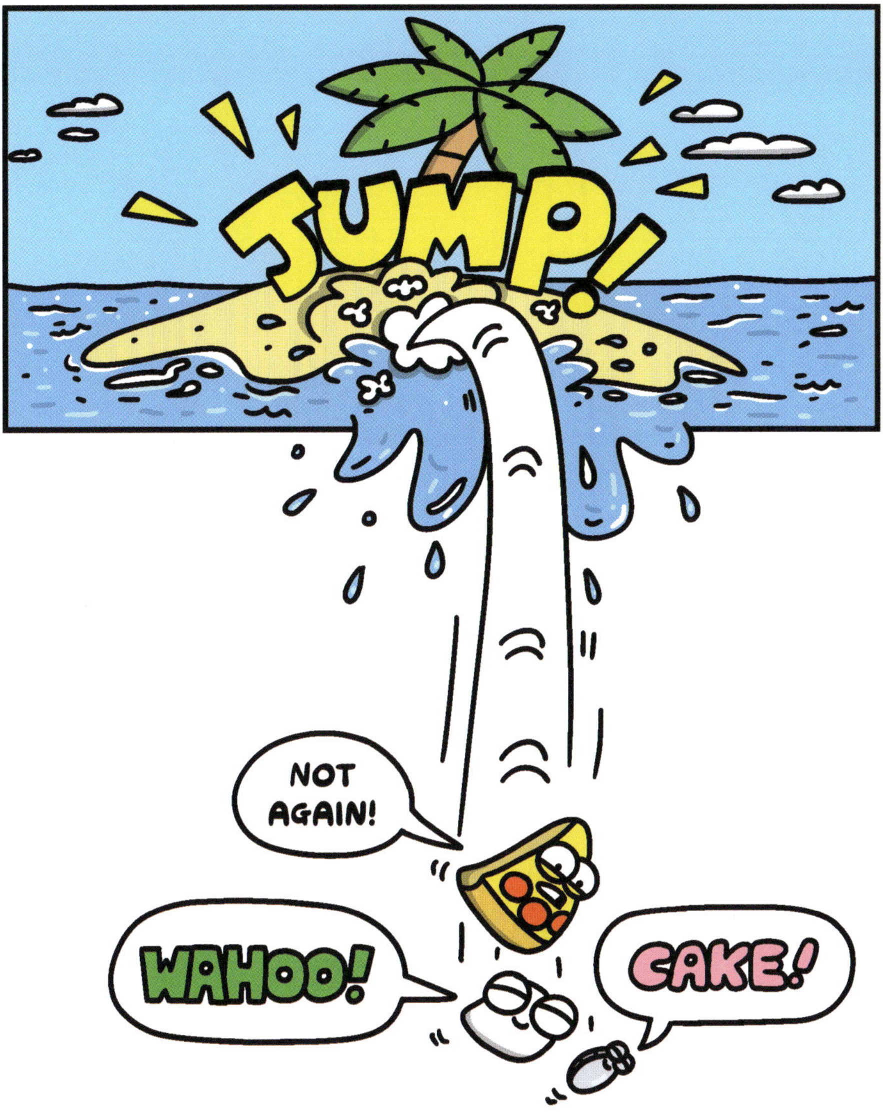
JUMP!
NOT AGAIN!
WAHOO!
CAKE!

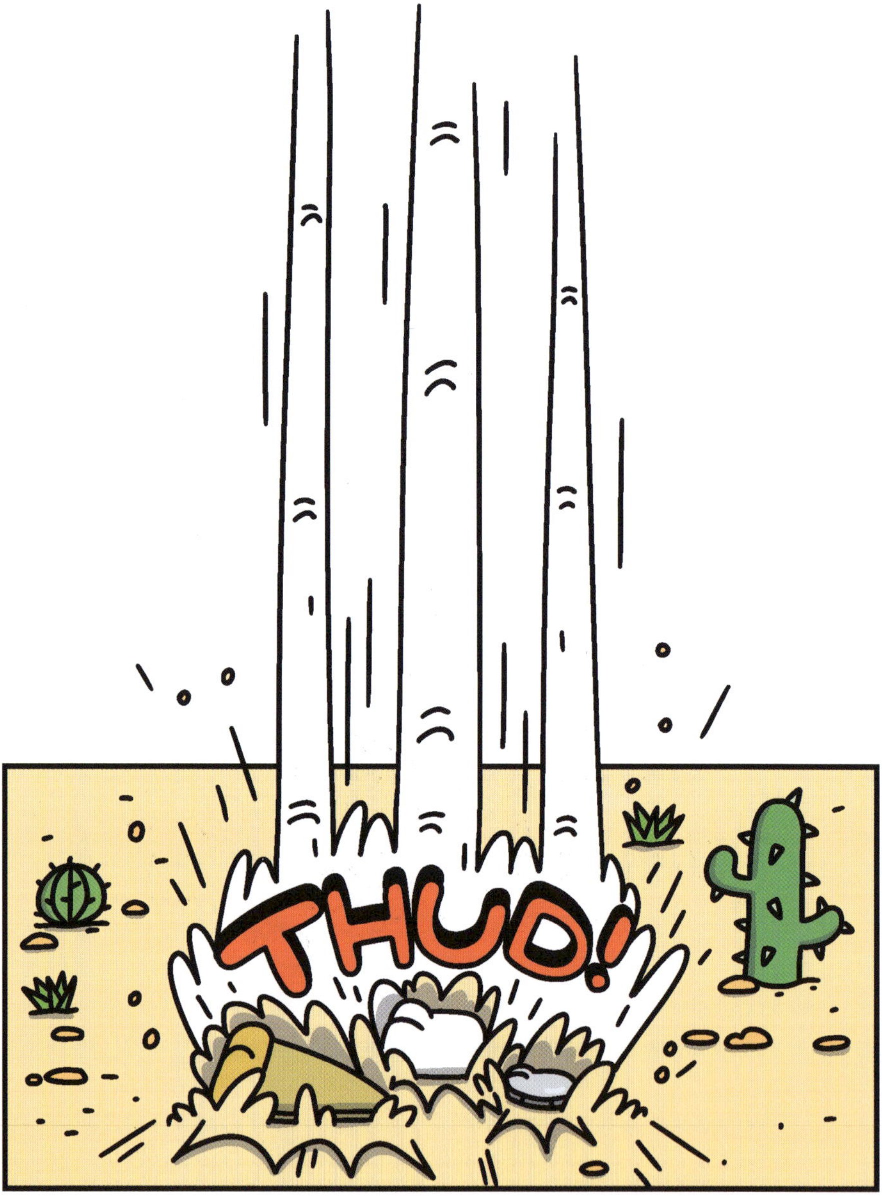
THUD!

WHERE ARE WE NOW?
IN THE MIDDLE OF A DESERT.
WHERE IS THE CAKE?
GREAT, WE'RE EVEN MORE LOST THAN BEFORE!
WHAT ARE WE GOING TO DO?
TOOT!
SIGH
GIGGLE
WASN'T ME.

WE COULD ASK FOR HELP?
GOOD IDEA! SOMEONE MIGHT KNOW THE WAY TO JELLY'S PARTY!
YEAH!
WHO CAN WE ASK?
WE'RE IN THE MIDDLE OF NOWHERE!

HELP!
WHY BOTHER SHOUTING FOR HELP WHEN NO ONE IS AROUND TO HEAR US?
ERR.
THAT WASN'T US, PIZZA.
WHOOSH!

SUPERHERO EGG!

WHO?

YOU'RE HERE TO SAVE US?

YAY!

SAVE YOU? NO...

SAVE ME!

FROM WHO?

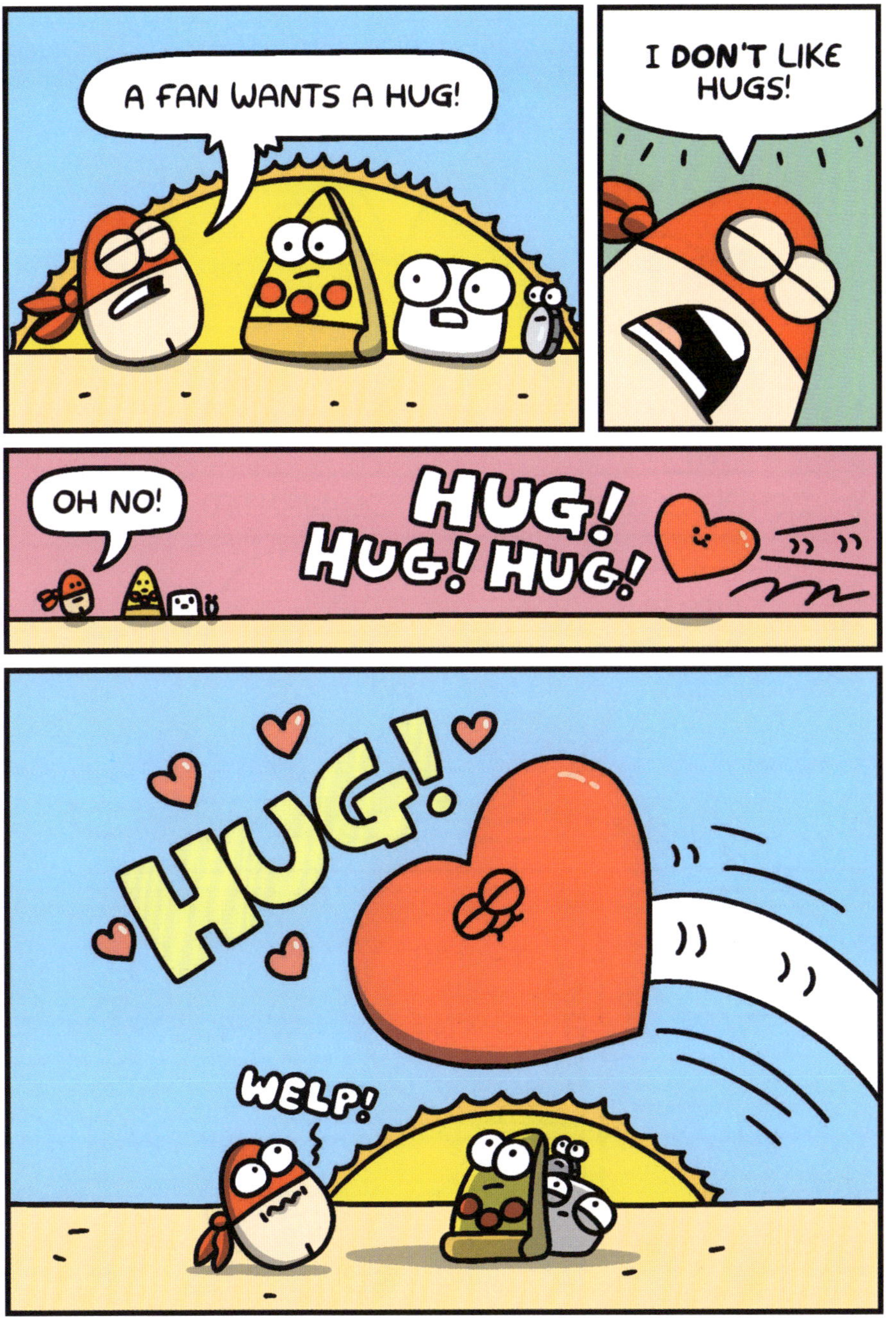
A FAN WANTS A HUG!
I DON'T LIKE HUGS!
OH NO!
HUG! HUG! HUG!
HUG!
WELP!

HUG!
GASP!
CRACK!
I SHOULD HAVE ASKED IF YOU WANTED A HUG.
I AGREE, ALWAYS ASK!
I'M SO SORRY.
THANKS FOR SAYING SORRY.

I'M SO LATE FOR JELLY'S BIRTHDAY PARTY!
WE ARE TOO!
CAKE!
WELL THEN, WHAT ARE WE WAITING FOR?
LET'S GO!

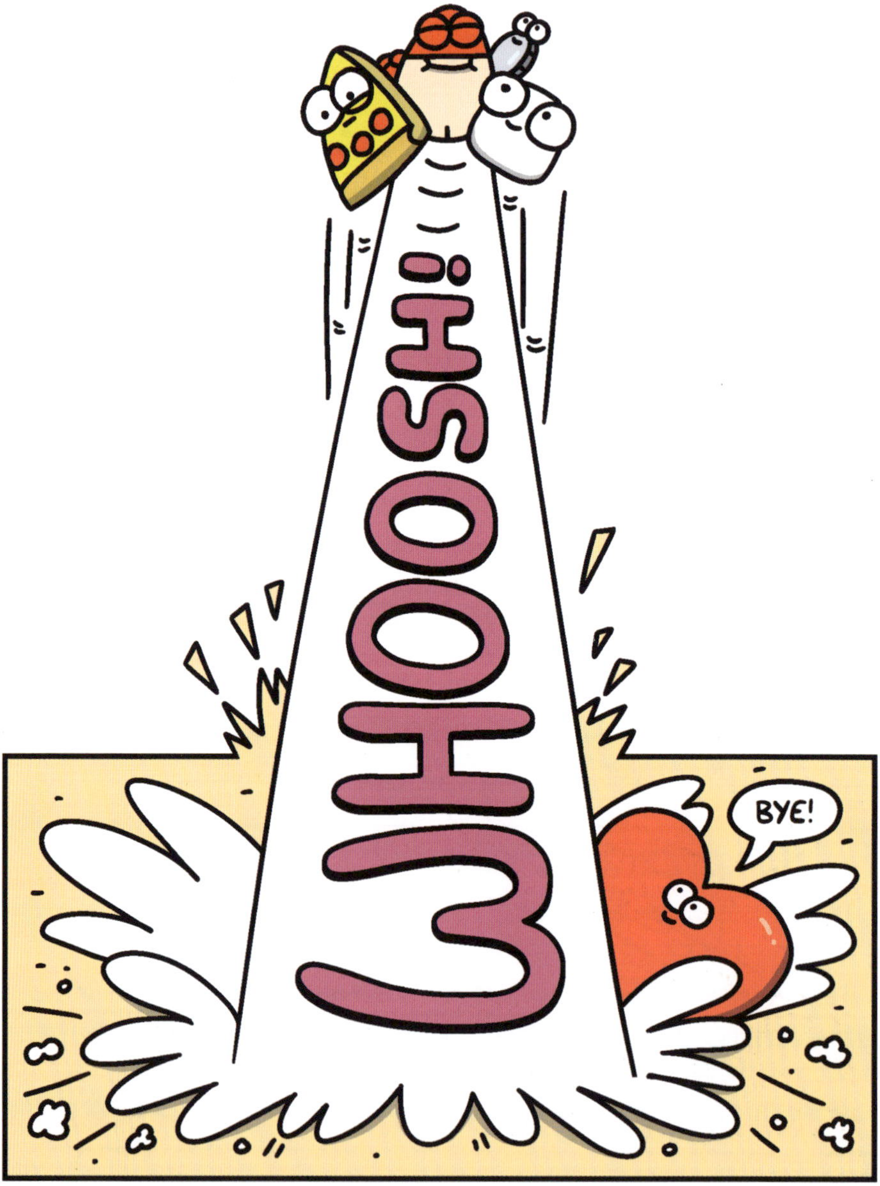
WHOOSH!
BYE!

NOBODY CAME TO MY BIRTHDAY PARTY!
SWOOSH!
SORRY WE'RE LATE!
THANKS SO MUCH FOR COMING TO MY PARTY!
I DIDN'T THINK YOU WOULD, BECAUSE...

I TRIED TO BE BETTER THAN YOU IN THE FIRST CHAPTER, TO GET MY OWN BOOK.

THEN, I BECAME A BAD GUY IN THE SECOND CHAPTER TO MAKE IT ALL ABOUT ME.

SO WHEN NO ONE CAME TO MY BIRTHDAY PARTY IN THE THIRD CHAPTER, I REALIZED I HAD BEEN A BAD FRIEND.

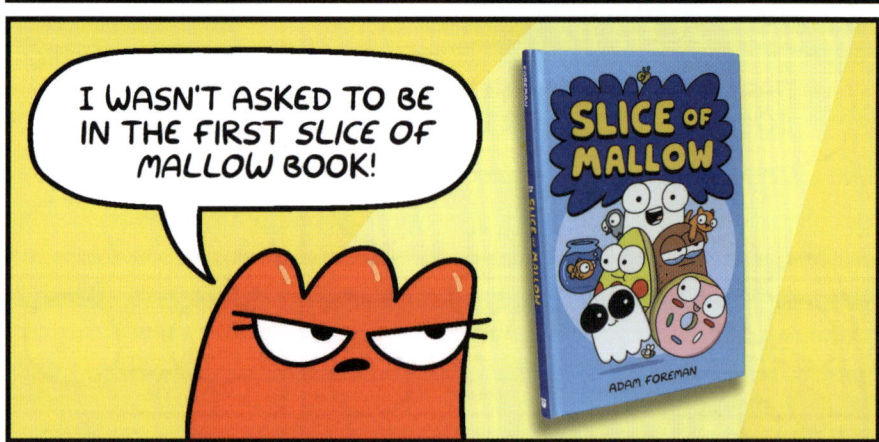

AND THE REASON?

I WASN'T ASKED TO BE IN THE FIRST *SLICE OF MALLOW* BOOK!

I'M SORRY.

HUG!

I'M SORRY YOU FELT LEFT OUT.

OH NO! POTATO, DOUGHNUT, AND GHOST HAVEN'T BEEN IN THIS BOOK.

I HOPE THEY DON'T FEEL LEFT OUT TOO!

ACTUALLY, WHERE ARE THEY?

I HAVE A FEELING WE ARE SUPPOSED TO BE SOMEWHERE.
SAME.
YUP.
SUPERHERO EGG RACING
GASP!
WHAT?
WE FORGOT TO BE IN THE SECOND *SLICE OF MALLOW* BOOK!
OH YEAH!
HAHA!

♡ HAPPY BIRTHDAY JELLY! ♡

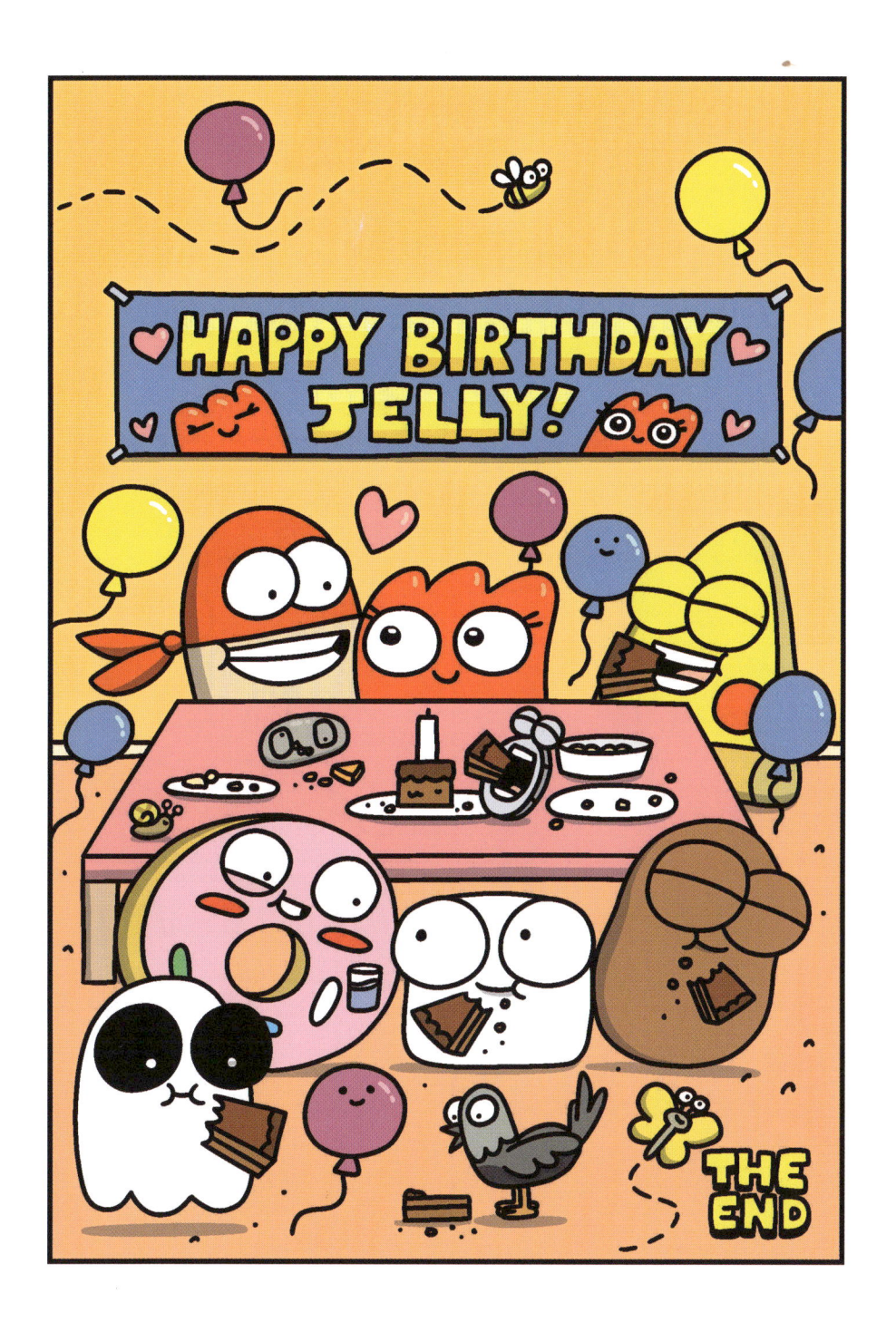

THE END

MEET THE AUTHOR / ARTIST
ADAM FOREMAN

ADAM CREATED THIS BOOK YOU'RE READING.

HELLO?

ADAM IS SCARED OF BUTTERFLIES.

WHAT?

NO I'M NOT!

AHHH!

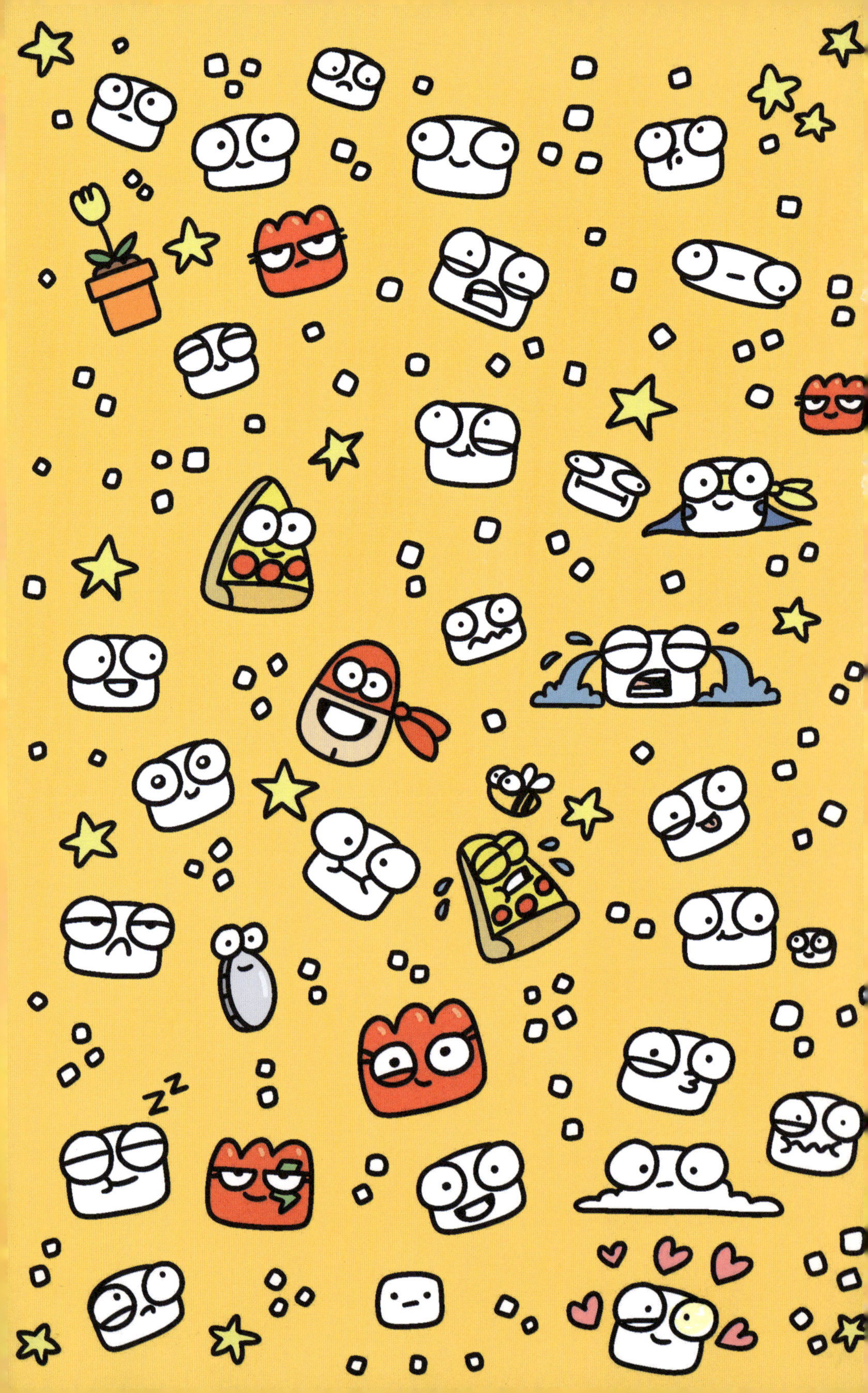